DONALD DU...
AND THE...

BASED ON THE MOTION PICTU... ...ATS"

TOLD BY ANNIE NOR... ...ORD

PICTURES BY THE WALT DISNEY STUDIO

ADAPTED BY DICK KELSEY

SIMON AND SCHUSTER • NEW YORK

THIS IS A BRAND-NEW BOOK, WRITTEN AND ILLUSTRATED ESPECIALLY FOR GOLDEN BOOKS

THE LITTLE GOLDEN BOOKS ARE PRODUCED UNDER THE SUPERVISION OF MARY REED, PH.D.

FORMERLY OF TEACHERS COLLEGE, COLUMBIA UNIVERSITY

Of all Walt Disney's merry characters, mischievous Donald Duck is by all odds the general favorite. His nephews have joined him in recent years, and in this new adventure they nearly steal the show!

It was getting on toward Halloween.

Donald Duck and his nephews were hunting for pumpkins for Jack-o-lanterns.

The day was almost over, and red and gold clouds were piling up in the sky, when they found a field that was full of pumpkins perfect for them.

They were walking back to the farm house, each with a round, ripe pumpkin in his arms, when Hughie stopped them all with a shout.

"Look! A witch on a broomstick!" he cried.
They all saw a dark form streak across the sky.

"Pooh!" said Donald. "Witches, pooh! There are no witches, you know that. It must have been some sort of a bird you saw."

But the boys were not convinced.

Next day they set out to look for the witch.
They had a long, hard walk through the tangled
woods. There was no path to follow, and they were
not even sure just what they hoped to find.

At last they heard a cackling laugh up ahead.
And what could be a surer sign of a witch than a
crickling, cackling laugh?

"Sh!" said Dewey, with his fingers on his lips.
And he led the way through the underbrush into
the clearing beyond.

There stood a crooked little house, clearly the home of a witch. From the crooked little chimney rose a thread of smoke.

Smoke and steam rolled up in clouds from a cauldron out in front. And through the smoke came that merry, scary sound, the cackling laugh of a witch.

"Welcome, boys, welcome," said the witch's
voice. "Welcome to Witch Hazel's little home."
Then she came hobbling toward them, a merry
little sprite, grinning with witchery glee.

The boys were speechless with surprise.

"What can I do for you today?" Witch Hazel
asked of them. "Any spells you'd like me to cast?
Anybody you'd like to bewitch?" And her elbow
poked Louie in the ribs, while she gave him a
sly wink.

"Bewitch!" echoed Louie.

"Cast spells!" said Dewey.

"Uncle Donald!" cried Hughie.

They all agreed. They told Witch Hazel how Donald refused to believe in her or any other witch.

"We'll show him!" she cackled, beckoning them close.

From the pockets of her dress she tossed bits of this and that into her steaming pot.

"A real witch's brew!" gasped Dewey Duck, as swirls of smoke in mysterious shapes began to rise and blow.

"We'll show that Donald!" Witch Hazel vowed. "You meet me here on Halloween."

Home went the boys, and they said not a word about their adventure to Donald Duck.

Donald was not surprised when the boys disappeared early on Halloween.

He was not surprised when his doorbell rang soon after dark that night. There beneath the porch light stood the boys. Donald chuckled as he recognized them through their disguises. They were dressed as witches, one and all.

"Come in," said Donald with a grin, holding his door open wide. They parked their broomsticks beside the door. (Donald rubbed his eyes as he thought he saw one jump. That, he knew, could not have been.)

In came the witches, one, two, three. No, there were one, two, three, four!

Donald was surprised, but he did not say a word as they all took seats around the room.

"Treats?" he asked, passing a tray of fancy little cakes.

"Ouch!" cried Dewey, who reached for one first. A mouse trap was stuck on his thumb.

"Wow!" cried Louie, who reached for one next.
It turned out to be a jack-in-the-box.

"Glub!" gulped Hughie, when he bit into his.
It was all made of rubber, you see.

"Thanks," said the fourth guest with a cackling
laugh. She blew at her cake, and it exploded into
dust, right in Donald's face.

"Serves you right, smartie," said a voice. Donald whirled around. There were only the Jack-o-lanterns sitting there, grinning saucily. But as Donald looked, it seemed to him that the merry faces shook with glee.

"We must be leaving now," one witch said. "Won't you come with us, and let us return your hospitality?"

"No, thanks," said Donald, clinging to the door-knob as they all swept him out onto the porch.

It was four against one. He soon found himself astride a broomstick.

"Abacadabra, boys! Here we go!" he heard a voice cackle in his ear.

All around him he saw broomsticks *fly*—and to his horror Donald saw the ground sink away below him too!

Over the treetops and straight toward the
moon the broomstick pointed — then down to the
woods.

"Welcome to Witch Hazel's little home," he heard the cackling voice say. And down tumbled Donald—down, down, down, into the witch's pot!

"Ho, ho, ho!" laughed the other three. He knew his nephews' voices all too well.

Donald gasped and sputtered. And he sizzled with rage when they hauled him out, soaking wet to the skin.

The witches did not notice. They were all doubled over, laughing fit to kill.

Witch Hazel disappeared into her little house, and came back with an extra dress and hat.

"Better put on something dry," she told Donald with a grin. And he stamped off into the house.

When he came out again, a table was set close beside the bubbling pot. Three Jack-o-lanterns glowed on a Halloween feast—pumpkin pie and apple tart and candy corn and all sorts of delicious things.

"Have a real treat, Uncle Donald," the nephews said, coming out from behind their masks.

So they all sat down and ate their fill—yes,
Witch Hazel too.

After a while, even Donald could smile.

"I still don't believe in witches," he said to Witch Hazel with a courtly bow. "But if there were any, I'd want them all to be just exactly like you."